# A Lizard's Tale

*by Beth Erlund*

**Erlund Johnson Studios**
COLORADO ✦ FLORIDA

A special thank you to **J4**, Tanzanian safari guide, for relating the happenings that inspired this story. In addition to providing me with an excellent view of the wonderful animals of Tanzania, he and the other guides gave us the adventure of a lifetime. Of course, none of this would be possible without the support and artistic guidance of my husband, **Dennis Johnson,** my editors **April Lucas** and **Jessica Egan** and the creative technical staff of **Greg Dunn** and **Karen McDiarmid.**

Inquiries about this book and prints of the batiks should be addressed to:
**Erlund Johnson Studios**
22528 Blue Jay Rd.
Morrison, Colorado 80465  USA
(303) 697-5188
www.erlundjohnsonstudios.com

Printed and bound January 2010, #52097,
Friesens of Altona, Manitoba, Canada.

Erlund, Beth
A Lizard's Tale / written and illustrated by Beth Erlund
SUMMARY: An encounter between a pride of lions and a monitor lizard
ISBN: 978-0-9762306-2-5
Library of Congress Control Number: 2009942448

Dedicated to all those
who face adversity
and come out winners.

One sunny morning in
the Serengeti,
the Simba family
was napping.

Mother and Father,
and all the aunts, uncles and cousins
had eaten breakfast.

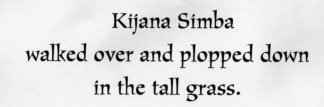

Kijana Simba
walked over and plopped down
in the tall grass.

He was bored.

Suddenly, Kijana saw
the monitor lizard, Kenge,
moving in the tall grass.
The lizard was moving toward a bone.
It was the leftovers from the Simba family breakfast.

Kijana got up and
marched right over to the lizard.
"Kenge!" he said.
"You are not a very smart lizard.
You are little compared
to ME."

"What is that lizard thinking?"
chirped a baby mongoose.

"Even a young lion is bigger than he is."
Mother mongoose said,
"He is a very brave lizard. Watch and see what happens."

A baby giraffe also saw Kenge.
She said to her mother,
"What is that lizard thinking?
The lions will not like him
trying to take some of their food."

Mother giraffe said,
"He is a very brave lizard.
We will have to wait
and see what happens."

Kijana reached out to push the lizard
away from the bone.

Before he knew what was happening,
Kenge's tail whipped around
and smacked
Kijana on the nose.

A surprised Kijana
jumped back and ran off
to get his mother.

"Mother! Mother! Come and see!"

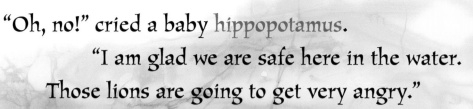

"Oh, no!" cried a baby hippopotamus.
"I am glad we are safe here in the water.
Those lions are going to get very angry."

Mother hippopotamus said,
"He is a very brave lizard.
We will have to wait
to find out what happens."

"That was not very smart," snorted a young zebra.
"The lions will surely get him.
What is that lizard thinking?"

Mother zebra said,
"He is a very brave lizard.
We will keep watching."

Mother lion followed Kijana over to the tall grass.
They circled Kenge, watching him eat.
Mother lion said, "Kenge, you are not a very smart lizard!
You are very little compared to ME."

She reached out to grab the bone away
but before she knew it, Kenge's tail whipped around
and smacked Mother lion's paw.
She jumped back in surprise.

Kijana went running to his father.
"Father! Father! Quick, come and see!"

"Should we run away fast?" asked a baby ostrich.
"What is  Kenge thinking?"
Father ostrich said, "He is a very brave lizard.
We will keep our eyes open in case of danger."

The young hornbill snapped,
"Doesn't that lizard know that
lions don't share their food with anyone?"
Mother hornbill said,
"He is a very brave lizard.
Watch and see
what happens."

A baby monkey heard the noise.
"What is that lizard thinking?" she worried.
"Lions will go after anyone who tries to take their breakfast."

Mother monkey said, "He is a very brave lizard.
We will have to wait and see what happens."

"Lions are the fiercest
animals in the Serengeti"
snorted a young rhinoceros.
"Doesn't that lizard know that?"

Mother rhinoceros said,
"He is a very
brave lizard.
Watch and find out."

Father lion followed Kijana
over to the tall grass.

He took one look at Kenge chewing on the bone and said,"
You are not a very smart lizard!
You are very, VERY little compared to ME."


He took two big steps toward the
lizard but before he knew what was happening,
Kenge's tail whipped around and
smacked Father lion's tail.

"There is sure to be trouble now!" chirped a young cheetah.
"What is Kenge thinking?"

Mother cheetah said, "He is a very, very brave lizard.
We will have to watch and see what happens."

The baby elephant trumpeted,
" I think now all the lions will chase him.
I don't think he can get away.
What is that
lizard thinking?"

Mother elephant said,
"He is a very,
very brave little lizard.
Yes, we will have to
wait and see what happens."

"Danger! Danger! Get ready to run!" squealed a young warthog.
"What is Kenge thinking?"

Mother warthog said,
"Stay here and find out what happens.
Kenge is a very,
very brave little lizard.

"Ha, Ha, Ha, Ha, Ha.
Kenge will not get away this time,"
laughed a baby hyena.

Mother hyena said, "Kenge is a very brave lizard.
Watch and learn."

Father lion was very surprised.
All the aunts, uncles and cousins quickly rose and
circled around Kenge.

They were loudly talking
to each other
about the foolish little lizard.

"Quiet! Quiet!" roared Father lion.
"Everyone be quiet. Let me speak."

"Kenge, you may be small and a little foolish,
but I also think
you are a very
brave lizard.
You were
hungry and
needed food."

"I think we all can learn a lesson from you.
Sometimes, even when you are afraid, you must take a chance.

Kenge, because you are so brave, you have earned the right
to share our breakfast. You may eat and no one will hurt you."


Quietly, Kenge said,
"Thank you," and finished his breakfast.

The morning in the
Serengeti was quiet and calm again.
The Simba pride went back
to their nap.

Kenge went on his way.

All the mongoose and giraffes,
the hippopotamuses and zebras,
the ostriches and hornbills,
the monkeys and rhinoceroses,
the cheetahs and elephants,
the hyenas and warthogs
and everyone else admired the
bravery of one little lizard.

Kijana curled up
next to his mother and his father and slept.
He dreamed that he was as brave as
a small monitor lizard.

*Moral: It doesn't matter how big or small you are
if you have bravery in your heart —
having a strong tail protecting you helps too!*

The End

## Monitor Lizard
*Swahili name: Kenge*

Monitor lizards grow 5 to 6 feet long. They use powerful tails to protect themselves. Even a small lizard's tail carries a sharp sting. They eat any leftover meat they can find in addition to snails, insects, other reptiles and birds. Like other lizards, the monitor likes to bask in the hot sun and can swim quite well.

## Cheetah
*Swahili name: Duma*

Cheetahs run at speeds up to 70 mph. They're the fastest land animal in the world. Cheetah mothers teach their cubs to hunt small antelope and mammals such as rabbits and birds. They do not roar, but growl, purr, and sometimes talk to each other using a chirping noise.

## Giraffe
*Swahili name: Twiga*

Giraffes have such long necks they must spread their front legs apart to drink water. Young can grow an inch a day. Leaves of the thorny acacia tree are a favorite food. They wrap their strong tongues around branches and pull off the leaves, leaving the thorns.

## Hippopotamus
*Swahili name: Kiboko*

Hippos are good swimmers who can stay under water for up to six minutes. They come out of the rivers at night to eat grass for 4 or 5 hours. Hippos have a flat paddle-like tail that they use to spread their poop in the water, marking their territory.

## Ground Hornbill
*Swahili name: Ngede (bird)*

Ground hornbills build nests in holes, on cliffsides, often in termite mounds. They eat insects, snakes and small mammals. They sleep in trees and need little water. Their faces are beige when they are born and slowly change to violet blue and red in females, and red in males.

## Rhinoceros
*Swahili name: Faru*

White rhinos have poor eyesight and often attack because they are not sure what they are seeing. They lower their heads, snort and run up to 30 miles an hour to batter their enemy with powerful horns. Birds called oxpeckers eat ticks from rhinos' skin and warn them of danger.

## Vervet Monkey
*Swahili name: Tumbili*

Ten to 50 vervet monkeys live together in trees, in groups called troops. Most of them are females and babies. Adult males move from troop to troop. They groom each other, picking ticks, fleas and dirt out of their hair. They mostly eat leaves, flowers, fruit and grass seeds.

## Dwarf Mongoose
*Swahili name: Nguchiro*

Twelve to fifteen mongoose live together in large, old termite mounds. They move often from one mound to another. They help each other hunt and babysit. They have keen eyesight and watch for enemies by sitting atop the mound, chirping when they see danger.

## Elephant
*Swahili name: Tembo*

African elephants (the largest land mammals) are known for their long, powerful trunks. The trunks are tools used for drinking, collecting food, dusting themselves and touching other elephants. They live in large herds. When there is danger, adults form a protective circle around younger elephants.

## Hyena
*Swahili name: Fisi*

Hyenas live in family clans and communicate with each other by the way they stand, calling to each other and making signals with their bodies. Sometimes it sounds like they are laughing. They eat meat and bones that they take from lions, leopards and cheetahs.

## Lion
*Swahili name: Simba*

Lions live and work in groups called prides — about 5 to 10 females, their cubs, and 2 or 3 males (usually brothers). Females are the hunters but males usually eat first, then females, and last, the cubs. Groups of lionesses can hunt large animals like hippos, zebra, giraffes, rhinos, young elephants and crocodiles.

## Ostrich
*Swahili name: Mbuni*

Ostriches are the largest living bird. They cannot fly, but they run fast. Ostriches have only two toes; the big toe has a nail that is like a horse's hoof and helps them run faster. They mostly eat plants. Since they have no teeth, they swallow small rocks to grind food in their gizzards.

## Warthog
*Swahili name: Ngiri*

Warthogs have large tusks and thick skin pads that look like warts. They hold their tails up high when they run, in part to help them stay together when they are in tall grass. They live in holes which they back into so that their tusks can protect them from their enemies.

## Zebra
*Swahili name: Punda Milia*

Zebras live in herds. Their stripes are their best protection from danger. The stripes of all the zebras together look confusing to lions and leopards. Mother zebras keep their babies close for several days after they are born so the babies will know the look, smell and sound of their own mother.

Africa

Serengeti

Swahili pronunciation key:
All vowels only have one sound,
similar to the Spanish
pronunciation of the vowel.

a as in taco
e as in egg
i as in igloo
o as in toe
u as in you

Words starting with m or n
followed by a consonant are pronounced with a
humming beginning on the m or n
followed by the rest of the word as in
"mmm-buni" or "nnn-dege".
With a little practice it is not hard.

**Batik:** an art media using wax and dyes to make a picture on cloth. Over 2000 years ago, the Chinese used beeswax and resin to make designs to decorate the fabrics that they dyed. Today, batik is created by drawing a pencil sketch on cloth and then drawing with hot beeswax and paraffin. The portions that are to remain white are drawn first, then the lightest dye is applied.

When the cloth is dry, wax is again applied to the portions that are to remain the color of the cloth and it is dyed again. This process is repeated thirty to forty times to achieve details for each color. Finally, the wax is removed and the picture can be seen in the cloth. During the dyeing process, the wax cracks and reveals little lines of color, adding the characteristic "crackle-look" that identifies the cloth as batik.

**Encaustic:** a mixture of beeswax, resin and pigments used to draw fine lines of texture atop a surface like batik. Heat is used to melt the mixture and fuse it to the surface.